For Gary, my "Let's Go!" guy—
thanks for all the world-travel adventures (so far)!
—R. G. G.

For Leo

—D. K.

First published in the United States of America in May 2018
by Bloomsbury Children's Books
www.bloomsbury.com

Bloomsbury is a registered trademark of Bloomsbury Publishing Plc

For information about permission to reproduce selections from this book, write to
Permissions, Bloomsbury Children's Books, 1385 Broadway, New York, New York 10018
Bloomsbury books may be purchased for business or promotional use. For information on bulk purchases
please contact Macmillan Corporate and Premium Sales Department at specialmarkets@macmillan.com

Library of Congress Cataloging-in-Publication Data
Names: Greene, Rhonda Gowler, author. | Kirk, Daniel, illustrator.
Title: Let's go ABC! : things that go, from A to Z / by Rhonda Gowler Greene ; illustrated by Daniel Kirk.
Description: New York : Bloomsbury, 2018.
Summary: Introduces the alphabet using a vehicle for each letter, from airplane to zeppelin.
Identifiers: LCCN 2017034338
ISBN 978-0-8027-3509-6 (hardcover) • ISBN 978-1-68119-946-7 (e-book) • ISBN 978-1-68119-947-4 (e-PDF)
Subjects: | CYAC: Vehicles—Fiction. | Alphabet—Fiction.
Classification: LCC PZ8.3.G824 Let 2018 | DDC [E]—dc23
LC record available at https://lccn.loc.gov/2017034338

Art created in Photoshop • Typeset in Archer • Book design by Danielle Ceccolini
Printed in China by Leo Paper Products, Heshan, Guangdong
2 4 6 8 10 9 7 5 3 1

All papers used by Bloomsbury Publishing, Inc., are natural, recyclable products
made from wood grown in well-managed forests. The manufacturing processes
conform to the environmental regulations of the country of origin.

LET'S GO ABC!

Things That Go, from A to Z

Rhonda Gowler Greene

illustrated by **Daniel Kirk**

BLOOMSBURY

NEW YORK LONDON OXFORD NEW DELHI SYDNEY

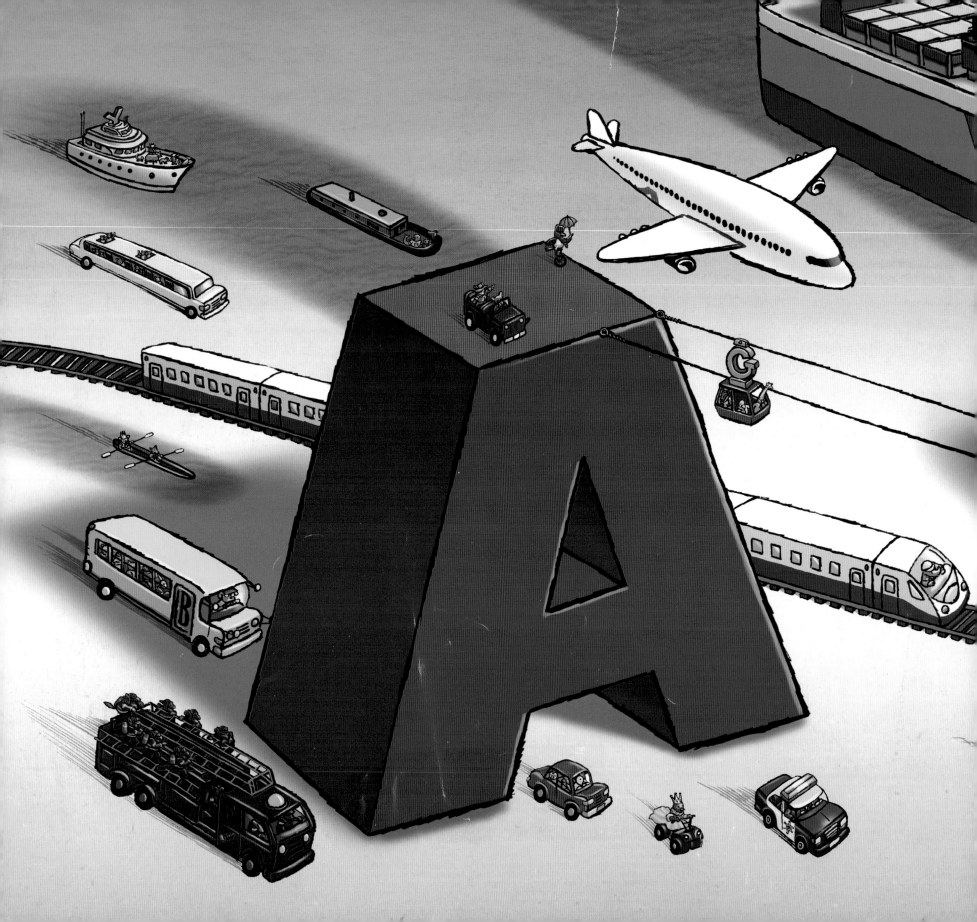

Need to get from here to there?
We can take you—*any*where!
On land or track, in air or sea,
we're transportation—A to Z.
Let's *GO!*

I pick up speed. I'm gaining height.
I catch the wind, ascend—in flight!
I'm an . . . Airplane!

I'm boxy-BIG, have rows of seats.
I bustle-bounce through busy streets.

Beep, beep!
I'm a . . . Bus!

On country curve or overpass,
I *vrrroom* along. I gobble gas.
And now I come electric, too.
Charge me up. Good as new!
I'm a . . . Car!

I go on snow.
I rush through slush.
By dog, I dash!
Huskies . . . *MUSH!*
I'm a . . . Dogsled!

Fearlessly, I race ahead.
My siren's LOUD! My lights flash red!
Thick smoke! And flames! Hoses? S-S-S-SPRAY!
I bring the team that saves the day!
I'm a . . . Fire Truck!

I glide you to a mountaintop.
What gorgeous views! Then, off you hop!
I'm a . . . Gondola Lift!

I'm a flying acrobat.
A spinning rotor is my hat.
I tilt . . . reverse. I hover, too.
Plus, I haul a rescue crew!
I'm a . . . Helicopter!

I sail by blade. I race on ice.
I'm first to cross the finish—*niiiice!*
I'm an . . . Iceboat!

I go by day, or night so starry.
Jump in! Join me on safari!
See that jaguar in the tree?
Explore! Come jungle-ride with me!
I'm a . . . Jeep!

One seat. Or two.
Ripples of blue.

A peaceful stream.
I kick back and . . . dream.
I'm a . . . Kayak!

I'm luxurious and looooong.
Your special night? Come roll along.
I'm elegant, and leisurely.
You'll feel just like a VIP. (*Very Important Person!*)
I'm a . . . Limousine!

I'm furious-fast! A mighty machine!
A bike with muscle—lean and mean!
I'm a . . . Motorcycle!

I'm a nimble, nifty gal.
I navigate through the canal.
I'm a . . . Narrowboat!

I'm big big **BIG**, yes, OVERSIZED.
Once on board, you'll be surprised
at all the fun you'll have on me—
a floating city on the sea.
I'm an . . . Ocean Liner!

I cruise through town out on patrol.
Protecting people is my goal!
I'm a . . . Police Car!

I'm quick and rugged, big-wheel rough.
Through quagmire, dirt, or mud—I'm tough!
I'm a . . . Quad Bike!

I aim toward space.
I *rattle-roar*.
Countdown . . .
Rumble . . .
Blastoff! . . .
Soar!
I'm a . . . Rocket!

Inside the sea, I whisper-sneak.
I'm sly. By periscope, I peek.
Shhhhh . . .
I'm a . . . Submarine!

T

Need a ride? Just wave me down.
Ta-da! Climb in. I weave through town.
For a fare I'll take you—*wheee!*—
exactly where you need to be.
I'm a . . . Taxi!

Try riding *me*. It takes technique.
And utmost balance! I'm unique.
I'm a . . . Unicycle!

I'm VAST. I voyage on the seas.
I make new-car deliveries!
I'm a . . . Vehicle Carrier!

Wait for me! I'm poky-slow.
I need a *pull* to make me go.
I'm a . . . Wagon!

Slower guys? I *swish* right past
because I'm eXtra, eXtra fast!

No stops for me . . . eXplode in speed!
My *click-clack*'s quicker, guaranteed!
I'm an . . . eXpress Train!

Yearn to *splish splosh* fancy-free?
I plow the waves in luxury!
I'm a . . . Yacht!

I fly without a zoom or zip.
Sail high! Come float by huge airship!
I'm a . . . Zeppelin!

SO many ways to move!
To *GO!*
By water, air,
through ice and snow,
by track,
by wheels upon a street,

or
maybe you prefer just . . .

FEET!

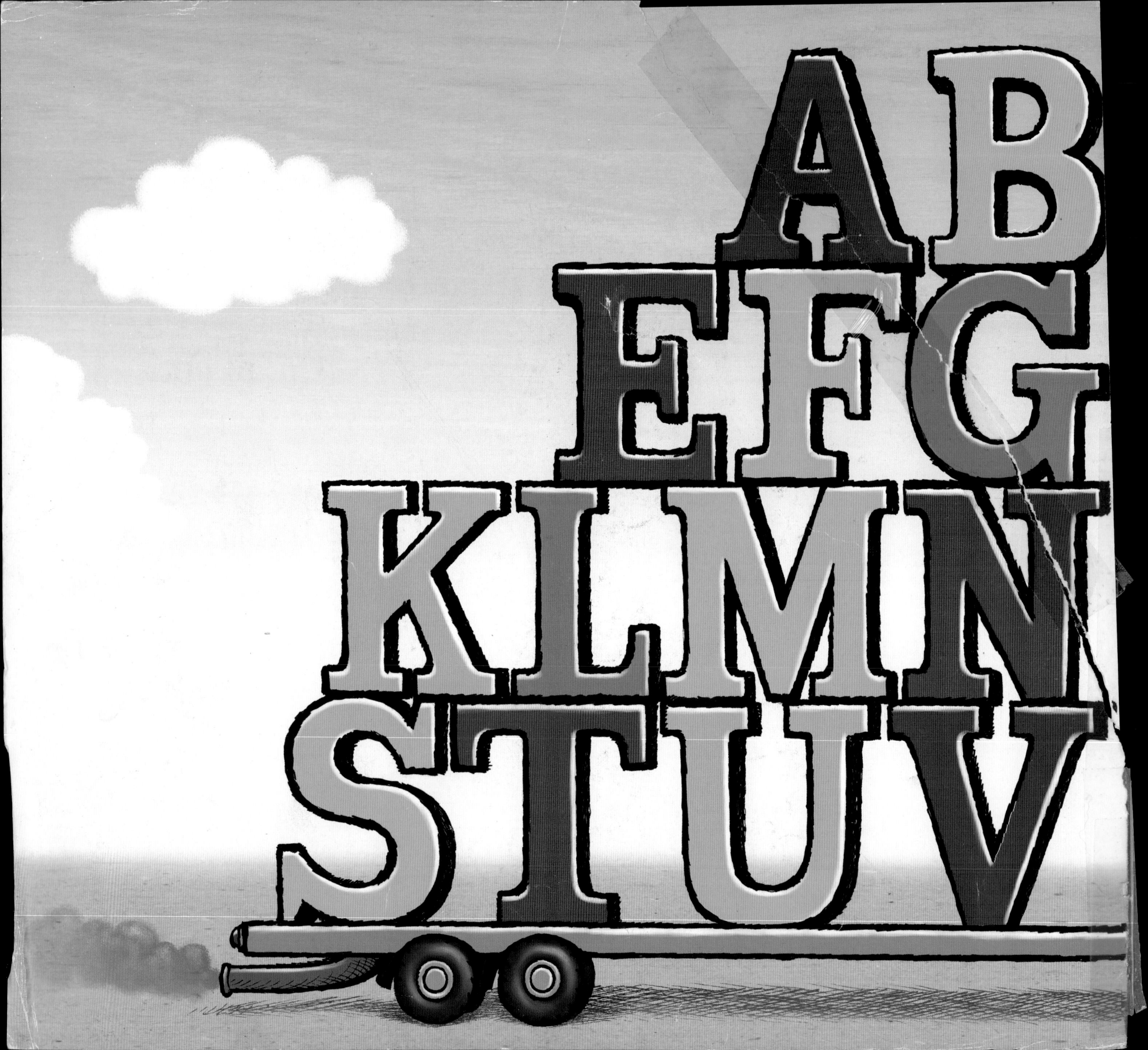
AB
EFG
KLMN
STUV